SCOUT and ACE

Flying in a Frying Pan

Written by Rose Impey
Illustrated by Ant Parker

ORCHARD BOOKS

Once upon a time, our heroes,

SCOUT and **ACE**

set out on a trip

into outer, outer-space.

Sucked through a worm-hole . . .

to a strange, new place,

lost in a galaxy called Fairy Tale Space.

It's a space-witch with
a mean-looking cat.
And she's flying in a frying pan!

Ace pulls a face and the witch's cat pulls one back.

Itty, bitty, kitty cat!

Now the witch has seen them.

"Look what you've done, you crazy cat!" shouts Scout.

"Come on!" squeals Ace.
"It's a race!"

Boom! **Boom!** ZOOM!

Scout and Ace zoom away.
And the witch zooms after them.

The witch has three tricks
up her sleeve.
First she throws her magic
hairnet after them.

The hairnet grows bigger...

and bigger...

until . . .

... it catches the spaceship.

"Yes!" squeals the witch.

But the SuperStar snips its way out.

Next the witch throws her magic comb after them.

The comb grows bigger . . .

and bigger . . .

until . . .

. . . it blocks the spaceship's path.

"Yes!" squeals the witch.

But the SuperStar saws
its way out.

Next the witch throws her
magic teeth after them.

The teeth come closer . . .

and closer . . .

until . . .

. . . they snap like a trap.
"Yes!" squeals the witch.
"Let's take those teeth
out," shouts Scout.

"Kapow!" says Ace. "Take that."

"Ow! Ow! Ow!" cries the witch
and her mean-looking cat.

The SuperStar zooms away.

And Scout and Ace live
to fight another day.

"Great race," says Ace.
But Scout looks cross.
"Keep your hairnet on, Captain,"
Ace tells him.

"No need to fly off the handle.
Broom! Broom!"
Scout groans. "Let's get out
of here," he moans.

Fire the engines...

and lower the dome.

Once more our heroes...

are heading for home.

Enjoy all these stories about

SCOUT and ACE

and their adventures in Space!

All priced at £8.99 each..

Colour Crunchies are available from all good bookshops, or can be ordered direct from the publisher:
Orchard Books, PO BOX 29, Douglas MM99 1BQ.
Credit card orders please telephone 01624 836000 or fax 01624 837033
or email: bookshop@enterprise.net for details.

To order please quote title, author and ISBN and your full name and address. Cheques and postal
orders should be made payable to 'Bookpost plc'. Postage and packing is FREE within the UK –
overseas customers should add £1.00 per book. Prices and availability are subject to change.

ORCHARD BOOKS, 96 Leonard Street, London EC2A 4XD.
Orchard Books Australia, 32/45-51 Huntley Street, Alexandria, NSW 2015.
This edition first published in Great Britain in hardback in 2004. First paperback publication 2005.
Text © Rose Impey 2004. Illustrations © Ant Parker 2004. The rights of Rose Impey to be identified as
the author and Ant Parker to be identified as the illustrator have been asserted by them in accordance with the
Copyright, Designs and Patents Act, 1988. A CIP catalogue record for this book is available from the British Library.
ISBN 1 84362 164 9   10 9 8 7 6 5 4 3 2 1
Printed in Hong Kong, China